INDI

SPENCER LAUREN YATES

Publisher iKAN Publish
INDI
Copyright © 2015 by Sheri Yates and Spencer Lauren Yates

This title is also available as a Kindle e-book.

ISBN-10: 1516839633
ISBN-13: 9781516839636

Cover and Interior Design: iPublicidades
Editor: Adam M. Swiger, Lee-Anne Weston-Ford
Wordsmith: Rebecca Bugger, Carrie White
Book Coaches: Sheri Yates, Elizabeth Ray, Stefne Miller
Cover Photo Credits: iKAN Shoot
Cover Photo Model: Chandler-Kate

iKANPublish.com
Printed in the United States of America

ACKNOWLEDGMENTS

This book was not easy to write. On the cover I am the acknowledged author, but without many people, my dream of writing a book would not even be possible.

Mom and Dad: Thank you so much for encouraging me to pursue my dreams, providing the resources, writing classes, and encouragement. Most of all, thank you for teaching me about Christ and showing His love through your actions. Without that, this book would not have even been a thought in my head.

Chandler and Kennedi: Thank you for motivating me and inspiring me when I became stuck. Thanks for encouraging me even when I thought the book was dumb and for always believing in me.

I would also like to thank two of my aunts, Elizabeth and Kathleen, who were both wordsmiths and editors. Elizabeth, thank you for spending your college summer break (when I was only nine years old) turning my thoughts into words and listening to my imagination run wild for hours and hours while you typed at a crazy speed. Thank you for your hours of research and for believing in me! Thank you,

Kathleen, for reading this over and over until you had it almost memorized. You have saved this manuscript from multiple typos.

Alex Schnee, thank you so much for being my first mentor. You inspired me never to quit, and after six years, my book is finally finished. Thank you for reading this book in its early stages, for sharing your wisdom and counsel, and for spending your time talking with me and encouraging me to press forward. Thank you for believing in Indi. Since you authored your first book at sixteen, but started it at nine or ten, I was inspired never to give up.

Stefne Miller, without you I would have never learned how to build my characters. Thank you for spending hours meeting with me and teaching me how to make a book interesting. Thank you for mentoring me.

Rebecca Bugger and Carrie White, I don't know what I would do without you. Thank you for dressing up my story and working countless hours writing and adding to the story. Thank you so much for what you do. I might have given up without you both.

Adam Swiger, thank you so much for being an excellent editor. For working through the book time and time again, searching endlessly for typos. You are very gifted in a way that I am not. I am very thankful for the work that you have put into this book.

INDEX

DEDICATION

This book is dedicated to my sisters, Chandler and Kennedi, my best friends, and also to every young person who has a dream. Never give up. If you're not failing, you're not trying.

Never give up. Ever. Never stop. I didn't wake up an author. I worked on this on and off over the past six years! Remain faithful to the work God has laid on your heart, and someday you will see it finished!

CHAPTER 1

GOOD MORNING!

Ganganagar, India

October 2001

"Mom, Dad! Don't leave! Who will take care of us? No, No!" she screamed, her voice hoarse with terror.

Suddenly there were hands on her arms, strongly clutching and shaking her. "Indi…Indi…Indi…Indi, wake up! Are you alright?" Indi was startled awake by her sister Englan's aggressive tone.

Indi shot up, and her eyes flew around the room in horror. *A dream,* she realized. It was all just a dream—a horrible dream. And there, at the side of her bed, was her six-year-old sister. She had heard Indi screaming and come to her rescue.

"I'm fine; I just had an awful nightmare," she said quietly. She was unsure where the dream had started, but she knew where it ended, and that ending was no place she *ever* wanted to be.

"Okay, well, you'd better get up because mama said your breakfast is getting cold." Englan bounced up and down on her bed, relieved.

That was odd, Indi thought. I haven't had a nightmare in so long that I forgot what they were like. I hope that never happens. I'd better hurry downstairs for breakfast.

She slowly made her way out of bed, settling her bare feet into the fake grass of the floor, and looked around at her wonderfully personalized room. She did not have regular carpet like other kids. Her daddy spoiled her rotten with all the extras a girl could dream of. Her room housed fuzzy grass-like flooring, a giant fake ladybug near the entrance, and a place for watching movies with her visiting friends. She would swing on the dragonfly — a ride shaped like a dragonfly connected to her ceiling. Next to the dragonfly was a trampoline in the shape of a mushroom, but of course it was fake and not a real mushroom at all. On the opposite side of the room was a real, living tree. Indi's dad had built her room around it. He was a very talented and creative man. The very middle of the room held an enormous flower, which she often climbed upon. Once she reached the top, she could slide down the plastic petals. In the middle of the flower was a round, yellow bed that she slept in every night.

Indi was nearly thirteen, but she still didn't feel too old to love her room and all its entertainments. Secretly, she truly loved being her daddy's little girl.

Her room was only one part of a wonderful house that her father had designed and built himself — three stories tall with a bell-shaped roof and unique, wonderful rooms for Indi, Englan, and their mother.

For himself, he had built an attic room with hundreds of shelves over all the walls for the family's many books. He loved reading, imagining, and creating things. The attic was also his home office, where he designed most of his blueprints for the houses he dreamed of building. Over the years, he had built many houses on the land around their home, surrounding a large courtyard where children would play.

He rented out some of the houses to make money and had even built a miniature playhouse especially for Indi and Englan. He had designed an extra-special kitchen for their mother, with a lot of cabinet space for her numerous kitchen tools, since she loved to cook, and he also had created a sewing room so she could create and sew all of the girls' clothes.

Their life was blessed, Indi knew for sure. They had money to build this kind of a house, food on their table every meal, servants, and so many other privileges. Most people barely had enough for necessities, let alone extra things.

Before her servant arrived, Indi hopped up to make her bed and room. Then her servant arrived to help Indi dress. She gathered her school things and headed out the door, through her butterfly tunnel hallway, toward the kitchen where her blistery cold breakfast was awaiting her sluggish body to get downstairs. She must have made a wrong turn somewhere, though, because she ended up in Englan's room instead.

She glanced about the room, nodding at the huge giraffe bed — which she sometimes pretended was a real giraffe. Its tail led to the second floor of the room, where there was a princess castle with many dress-up dresses. Indi realized that Englan's cat, Whitney, was not in the room, which probably meant that Englan was carrying her around as usual. Englan had even begged their daddy to build a miniature version of her room just for that crazy cat.

Since her sister wasn't in her room, Indi turned and ran downstairs for breakfast. On the way downstairs, she noticed a servant about her age, one of the many in the house, on her way upstairs to make Indi's bed. Indi stopped her quickly, "There's no need to make my bed; I already did."

The gentle servant nodded with a smile. "Thank you, miss." She turned to finish her other chores.

Finally, Indi made it downstairs, famished and ready to eat. She could smell the sweet aroma of scrumptious food. Her stomach growled while her mouth watered. She turned into the kitchen to find a strange man on a ladder. He was so high up that she had to stretch her neck to figure out what he was doing. In the middle of the hallway that led to the kitchen was a beautiful chandelier that her father had designed. The man was changing the light bulbs and tightening bolts.

When she caught his eye, he curled his long mustache up with a creepy grin. Indi attempted to ignore the chills that ran down her spine as she managed to smile back in his direction. She briskly walked into the kitchen.

Her father had built her mother a wonderful kitchen, and the food that came from it was always rich, sweet, and mouth-wateringly savory. She lingered over the buffet line so she wouldn't miss any of her mother's delicious food. Her grin increased from ear to ear as she gazed across the many bowls of sausage, eggs, biscuits, mashed potatoes, fried potatoes, baked potatoes, grilled potatoes, and toast. Breakfast was her all time favorite meal — well, at least until lunch, and then dinner.

She heaped scoops of food onto her plate and wondered whether she would be able to eat it all.

Finally, she sat down at the table to join her family. Her parents spoke quietly to each other. It was rude to interrupt adults, so she patiently waited until her parents were finished and then spoke up.

"Mom, Dad, I had a nightmare last night, and I'm...well...I'm kind of...afraid."

"What are you afraid of?" her mother asked gently, leaning forward to put a hand on Indi's arm.

"I'm afraid you will die soon and leave me alone to care for Englan!"

"Die? Us? Soon? That would never happen!" her mom reassured her.

"Let's change the subject," her dad urged. "Are you ready for school?"

"Yep. I have my backpack right here."

She looked closely at them, still wondering about her nightmare, but decided that they were probably right. Nothing would happen. They had the most wonderful life in the world and loved each other so much. Things would never change. She ate in silence, shoveling the scrumptious food into her mouth. As soon as she was done, she jumped up, ready for school. She hugged her parents and raced out the door. After a couple of steps, though, Indi stopped and turned back.

"Oh, wait…" She bounded back through the door and bent low to hug her little sister. "See you after school, Englan!" she shouted as she ran to meet her friends.

Englan eagerly watched them until they disappeared down the dusty road.

CHAPTER 2

FRIENDS

Indi's School in Ganganagar, India

Same Day, October 2001

The bell rang, and Indi and her friends, Olivia, Georgeann, Victoria, and Clem, pulled out their books and scooted their desks closer together. They had been friends ever since Indi could remember. They talked about everything — clothes, dishes, shoes, books, animals, plays, and a whole variety of other things — but on this particular day, they were talking about something super important: *homework*.

"I can't believe that we have to do homework on paper. It just wastes the beautiful trees!" Indi muttered, frustrated.

"I don't mind. I'm personally not a huge fan of trees," Victoria answered sharply.

Olivia slouched in her seat. "Besides, what would we write on if we didn't use paper, Indi?"

"Bark?" Clem suggested.

Georgeann rolled her eyes. "That wastes trees, too."

Just then, Mrs. Brooke, their teacher, gracefully stepped into the room. "Good morning, class."

"Good morning, Mrs. Brooke," the class chanted in unison.

School had now begun, and Indi leaned forward with her pencil poised to take notes. She glanced to the side and noticed that Clem had already fallen asleep. Again. Her head was down on the desk. Indi wondered when Mrs. Brooke would notice, but Olivia poked at Clem and successfully woke her up. Indi accidentally snorted with laughter. Clem was always getting them into trouble.

Indi continued to take notes. She was in the middle of outlining a short story for their next writing assignment when a ruckus broke out in the classroom. Mrs. Brooke briskly strode down the aisle, and Indi thought she heard a furious scuffling behind her desk. Before she could determine what had happened, the teacher arrived and quickly snatched something out of Clem's hand. A note, Indi realized. Clem had been passing notes again. Again.

Mrs. Brooke flipped the note open and eyed Clem sharply. "A note to Victoria, I see," she said sternly. "And what is so important that it could not wait until after class? Oh, let me read." She scanned the contents of the note, then laughed and handed the note to Victoria. "It seems our friend Clem would like your help with math, Victoria," she said in a singsong voice. "I can't fault her there. In the future, though, I suggest you wait to ask her in your free time."

She turned and glided gracefully back to the front of the classroom, leaving a wake of laughter behind her. Indi glanced at Clem, chuckling, and then continued outlining her story.

Before long, lunch had arrived. Lunch was Indi's all time second favorite meal after breakfast; then came dinner, of course. But it wasn't so great today because an argument broke out among her friends.

"Vicky, if you had been quicker getting to that note, then I could have hung out at recess with you guys! But now I have to clean the classroom!"

"It's your own fault! You could've gotten me into some serious trouble, Clem, if I had been caught helping you cheat!" Victoria snapped.

"She is right; you are the one who wrote the note," Georgeann agreed.

Clem stuck out her lower lip. "You guys always blame me! And I wasn't asking you to help me cheat. I just needed help!"

"Don't pout. I'm the one who saved you when you were about to be caught sleeping!" Olivia snapped. "You really should be more careful, Clem."

"Let's not waste our time, girls. We only have a couple minutes left," Indi urged.

There was silence, and Clem sadly followed the rest of the group, forgetting she was supposed to return to clean the classroom. Once outside, they found that the principal had read the note in question and considered it much more serious than Mrs. Brooke had. She was waiting for them and hustled Clem directly to her office.

"I knew this would happen!" Olivia exclaimed.

"You know, Olivia, you shouldn't constantly expect trouble!" Georgeann scolded.

"Guys, we're always fighting! Stop it! It wastes our precious time together," Indi exclaimed. She was putting her foot down this time.

"Indi's right," Victoria agreed. "There's nothing we can do about it now. Clem is in who knows what kind of trouble. We just have to hope that we don't get into trouble, too. Fighting won't help anything."

Olivia twisted her hair. "I guess so," she admitted.

"Let's just jump rope and think this through," Georgeann suggested.

So the girls jumped rope during their recess. The soft pitter-patter of the rope, the trees swaying from side to side, and the yellow, orange, and red leaves falling from the trees made it seem like a fairytale. Winter was coming. Indi knew that meant long nights inside, listening to the rain. In stormy weather, all the girls hung out at her house to play in her spectacular room or play games in front of the vast fireplace with her parents. In truth, her friends were more like sisters to Indi and Englan, and they loved Indi's parents almost as much as she did. Her mother was teaching them all to quilt. Though Indi loved summer most, the long, quiet nights of winter were special, too. She glanced up at the sky, wondering if it would rain soon, and began to think happily about the quilt she would design next.

In the principal's office, Clem was thinking much darker thoughts. She knew that she was in huge trouble but wasn't sure just how much trouble. *I hope I'm not suspended. Why am I always getting into trouble? What will I say? I know! I'll just tell her the truth*, she thought.

"Excuse me. Clem?" the principal uttered.

Mrs. Brooke walked out, leaving the principal and Clem alone.

Clem's heart pounded — so loudly that she assumed her friends at recess could hear it.

"I am very disappointed in your recent behavior," the principal continued. "I'm sure you have an explanation."

"Well, you see, I just forgot what I was doing and followed my friends outside. I didn't remember that I was supposed to clean the classroom."

The principal frowned, her brows coming down over her eyes. "May I please have the truth?"

"But…that is the…truth."

The principal sighed. "Clem, I'm talking about the note. It's clear to me that you were asking Victoria to help you cheat, and that is against our school policy. Mrs. Brooke might not recognize the severity of this, but that is because she is overly kind to you. I think you need some time to think about this." Then she paused. "You are suspended for three days. Use this time to evaluate your behavior."

Clem was devastated. *Three whole days? Did that just happen? What will my friends think? Will they even want to hang out with me anymore? Maybe I'll have to live the rest of my life by myself with no friends! Oh, quit stressing yourself out! You've got to think this through thoroughly. Would my friends actually abandon me? Maybe…No! They wouldn't.*

"Dismissed!" the principal announced.

What did she just say? Clem must have been in such deep thought that she didn't hear the principal's words.

The principal looked annoyed. "Must I repeat myself?" she asked. "Dismissed!"

Clem walked solemnly out the door, down the empty hallway, through the faded yellow grass, and onto the dirt road toward home.

The whistle blew, which meant it was time for the schoolchildren to make their way inside, back to their classrooms. For the rest of the day, Indi, Georgeann, Olivia, and Victoria worried about Clem. She had not returned to class. That was surely not a positive sign.

Maybe they sent her home for the rest of the afternoon. Or maybe she's still at the principal's office. I'll know when she walks home with us later, Indi thought nervously.

Whatever it was, surely it couldn't be that awful. Clem reaped her share of trouble, but so far it had never been *too* serious. This time would likely be more of the same.

When they gathered at the front of the school after the last bell rang, however, Clem did not join them. The girls waited, staring hard into the hallways and offices of the school, but there was still no Clem.

Finally, after they had waited for nearly half an hour, Victoria turned to the others. "I am worried about Clem! Has anyone heard anything about where she is?" she asked quietly.

Olivia — always the sarcastic one — answered sharply, "Of course we know where she is!"

"You do?" Victoria wanted to know.

"Of course not, silly!" Georgeann answered. "How would we know where she is?"

"She's not here anymore," Indi answered finally. "If she were here, she would have come out by now. We have to find her. Her house is on the way home. Let's stop there to investigate. If she's not here, she just must be at home."

They turned as one like soldiers, all in agreement with this plan, and marched down the street toward Clem's house.

CHAPTER 3

UNEXPECTED

Clem's House

When they arrived, they saw that the house was tall, dark, dreary, and rather shabby. Indi was surprised; she had never been invited to Clem's house, and now she began to understand why. She had never realized that her friend lived in a house like this. What else did she not know?

Victoria looked disgusted. "Is this really Clem's house? It's not how she described it — at all!"

Indi skipped up the steps, ignoring Victoria's statement, and lightly knocked on the door. When it opened, a little girl who smelled of cigarette smoke stood on the other side.

"Whadya want?" the girl asked impolitely.

"We would like to speak to Clem Kane, please," Indi replied.

The girl rolled her eyes. "C'mon in. Clemmy's upstairs."

The four of them walked in and took a look around. The floor was covered with dirt, the ceiling had several holes in it, the walls were bare, it was hot and stuffy, and there were no windows in the entire large room. It looked like a very miserable place to live. The girls lingered for a moment, then made their way up the filthy stairs. There were so many depressed-looking children everywhere — more than Indi could begin to imagine in one family.

Were they all related to Clem? What was this place? Indi hungered to help but wasn't sure where to start. Certainly she couldn't clean the whole place! They needed to find Clem and ask for details. Where were her parents? Was there anyone in charge here?

Once upstairs, Indi spotted Clem, who was curled up in a corner with her face in her hands. Indi was the first to approach Clem. She gently sat down beside her. It was obvious that her friend had been sobbing.

"Clem — what's the matter?"

Clem looked up in time to observe softhearted Indi bending over her, wiping her eyes. "Nothin'," she replied.

Indi smiled. "You weren't at school, and you have been crying. I know there is something wrong."

Clem suddenly noticed all her other friends standing awkwardly by her bed. Indi gestured for them to enter into their little huddle, so the girls slowly approached the tiny corner. Clem was a bit embarrassed and ashamed; it didn't take an expert to realize that.

"Let's leave this place and walk over to my house," Indi suggested, finally breaking the silence. She believed that if this were her house, she certainly wouldn't want people visiting. Besides, Indi's mother and father would be home soon, and dinner should be ready. It was time for her father to start talking about his day and sharing stories about the houses he had worked on. If that didn't cheer up Clem, nothing would. "We'll have dinner, and you can tell us what happened in the principal's office," she finished.

Clem tried to smile, but through her tears she just nodded. "Sounds good to me."

CHAPTER 4

INDI'S HOUSE

Everyone attempted to walk quickly, but sorrow weighed them down. Indi wanted to know what had happened in the principal's office more than anyone else since she and Clem had been friends the longest.

It didn't take her long to speak up. "Clem, we all *need* to know what's wrong."

"Because we care about you, Clem!" Olivia added.

"Why were you in that filthy house? And why were you crying in the corner?" Victoria blurted out question after question without giving Clem a chance to answer.

Clem lifted her chin and faced the curious girls. "The first thing you ought to know about me is that I'm no ordinary girl." She paused. "My mom and dad both died in a car accident when I was only three years old. I had no godparents, so I became an orphan on the street.

"Then Ms. Amberlee, the orphanage headmaster, found me and brought me into the home. The first few days were some of the best days of my life. But on my fourth day, I learned the rules, and…they were harsh. Ms. Amberlee expects the children there to be the best at everything, and if you do anything wrong in school, you have to deal with her wrath. Today you found me crying because the principal sent me home for three days' suspension from school so that I could think about what I did. Guys…I am suspended! I'm afraid that Addigail, the meanest bully at the orphanage, will rat me out to that old grouch Ms. Amberlee. When she finds out, her meanness will be comin' at me hard. "

They were at Indi's house by the time Clem had finished the story. They all paused, processing everything Clem had said, and strolled inside without asking any more questions.

Indi was shocked to hear this news. How long had she known Clem and yet never realized that the girl was an orphan? *I am a horrible friend. How terrible not to know your parents and not to know that someone loves you!* Indi's thoughts raced.

That made her remember her dream, and she gasped. Just then, though, her mother walked into the kitchen.

"Oh, you're just in time!" she shouted cheerfully. "Indi, can you watch Englan while I go out?"

Georgeann smiled. "We'll all watch her, Mrs. Hudson."

Indi's mother started walking toward her car. "Perfect! I would love to chat with you sweet girls, but I need to leave now or I will be late."

Indi's mom worked as a part-time dressmaker. Not because they needed the money but because she was extremely talented and enjoyed the work. Indi watched Englan every day after school so that her mother could do fittings and things.

It was Indi's dad who worked the best job, though, and he earned all the money for the family. He, of course, was a house designer, and an excellent one at that. He designed the most beautiful houses and had built most of the homes in their city. He and Indi's mother desired to travel, though, and had always dreamed of visiting other cultures. That was, after all, how Indi had been named. Her mother, Chine, had come from a family with a tradition that each child in every generation was given the name of a place from around the world. For instance, Chine's name was from China, Indi's name was from India, and Englan's name was from England. Her father, Thomas, did not come from a family with this tradition, so he just had an ordinary name. Both Chine and Thomas were born and raised in England, but once they were married, they moved to the beautiful land of India. Indi was born there. Seven years after Indi, Englan was born. Six years had now passed, and they were happy.

Indi nodded to her mother as she departed, still dazed at the news she had just heard from Clem. She found her sister first. It was nice outside, but the servants had already built a ragingly warm fire in the living room. She ushered her sister and friends to the sitting area and gazed around at them.

"Clem? Is something wrong?" Englan asked shyly.

"No Englan, not anymore," Clem replied.

Indi thought for a moment, wondering whether Clem was actually as calm as she appeared. What her friend needed, she thought, was a distraction. Walking to the lake with Englan was not an option, and she was certainly not in the mood for quilting that night. Finally she hit on a decent idea. "How about we ride on the dragonfly ride?" she asked.

Everyone agreed, so the girls made their way upstairs. Once in

Indi's room, Clem climbed onto the dragonfly, the other girls trailing behind her. Clem hopped on the ride and reached down to help up Englan, and the other girls followed. Once everyone was seated, Indi started the ride, and it made a loud booming noise.

"Boom!" Englan shouted, copying the ride. The other girls laughed and buckled their seat belts, ready to enjoy the swift turns around the room.

When they were ready, Indi pushed another button, and the ride shot forward, then backward, and climbed higher and higher. Englan screamed the whole time, but that was nothing new; she always wanted to ride the dragonfly and then decided that it was terrifying halfway through. Victoria's eyes were huge, and Olivia squealed while Georgeann and Indi laughed. But Clem just remained still while watching the others.

When they were finished, Englan asked her, "Clem, is there anything you're afraid of?"

"Bullies," Clem answered.

"You must be a brave person 'cause you're braver than me, and Mama says that I'm very brave," Englan awed.

Indi watched Clem closely and wondered how brave the girl actually was. Then again, she was living without parents in a dirty, rundown building. That took more courage than Indi had known her friend had.

Once her parents arrived home, they all ate dinner as quickly as possible, barely listening to Mr. Hudson's account of his day. They all desperately longed to continue their conversation with Clem. After dinner, Indi and her friends were given permission to walk to the lake.

Most nights after dinner, Indi and her friends hung out together by a small pond they called "the lake." The lake seemed like the only place they experienced pure fellowship.

When they arrived, the sun was just starting to sink toward the horizon, and the water was shining brightly, reflecting the sun's gorgeous light. The soft breeze carried the waves to and from the shore, and Indi turned her face toward the sun, closing her eyes and enjoying the brisk air on her cheeks.

"So whatcha wanna do?" Clem asked suddenly, hopeful that she could get the subject off of her.

Georgeann gave Clem a look. "It's pronounced, 'So what do you want to do,' and I think I can answer that question for you. How about we either sit and look at the sunset or swim?"

"How 'bout we build a sand castle?" Indi suggested. Although she loved swimming, she didn't feel like getting wet when the air was so chilly.

Everyone agreed to the sand castle, so they began pushing sand into a massive pile. The pile of sand soon began to grow taller and wider — until it was so huge that not even the tallest of them could reach the top. Everyone worked together, and the bottom of the castle slowly formed. As time passed and darkness approached, the girls worked at a steady pace. Before they knew it, the mountain of sand had turned into a glamorous castle. They built walls and turrets and larger buildings with sloping roofs and even flags. When they finished working on the outside of the castle, the girls began shaping the inside. It was the most enormous castle that they had ever built, and Indi was the designer of it. She had studied her father's blueprints. She secretly loved being like her daddy.

Soon after they had started, the inside of the castle was complete. It was so massive that it could fit all the girls inside. They stepped back to enjoy their wonderful masterpiece. Olivia peeked at the others to make sure no one was looking. As it turned out, the others were doing the same. All at once, the girls rushed through the wee opening of the human-sized castle, shrieking with excitement. All of them could squeeze in there together, and they played and laughed until darkness overshadowed them and their mothers called for them to come home. Indi and her friends rushed back to their houses, full of laughter and delight.

Clem, who had no mom to call her in, wandered around for a bit and then found her own way home.

CHAPTER 5

DADDY-DAUGHTER DATE

Late December 2001

Time passed quickly for Indi after that, and she never thought about Clem's situation again. Clem returned to school, and the girls continued in their happy, carefree existence. The days grew shorter with winter, and they spent more and more nights at Indi's house by the fireplace, telling stories and learning to knit. Then one day, when summer was finally returning, Indi's dad asked an unusual question.

"Indi, would you like to join me for a daddy-daughter date?"

Indi's mouth fell open. "Of course, Daddy! How could I say no?"

He smiled. "Is that a yes, then?"

"Of course I say yes!" Indi exclaimed, excited.

So it was decided that they would have their daddy-daughter date at the nearest daddy-daughter dance competition. They knew it would have American music, but they had no idea how modern the songs and dances would be. Indi chose the easiest dress to dance in, her nicest calico, and comfortable, flat dancing shoes. Her father chose something a little more modern for the occasion — nice, clean, and crisp pants; a white, dressy shirt; and a black jacket with a red and black striped tie.

When they arrived, many American girls danced with their dads. All the dads, except Thomas, were merely wearing jeans and a t-shirt. Indi and her daddy were certainly overdressed for the competition, but they wouldn't let that bother them.

Indi and Thomas observed for a while to learn some dances, but then they joined in and proceeded to dance all night long. Although Thomas and Indi were kind of out of place, they had a blast. Indi hoped there would be another daddy-daughter date in the near future. She loved both of her parents, but there was never enough time with her dad, who had to work. Work. WORK.

Her mom, on the other hand, stayed at home to take care of Indi and Englan, but it had always been her daddy who put them to bed, tucked them in at night, and made up stories when they couldn't sleep. She tried to contain her wild imagination from thinking about how she could ever live without either of her parents.

CHAPTER 6

EVERYTHING CHANGES

Early January 2002

Only one week after the daddy-daughter date, everything changed. Indi's father brought home the most shocking news: he had lost his job. His company — that he had worked for and built so many beautiful houses in the city with — was closing, and with the company went Thomas's job.

"I believe I could stay here and start my own company, but what if that failed?" he asked, gazing at Chine, then at Indi and Englan. "I could not bear it if something happened."

Indi's mother reached out to lay a hand on his cheek and turned to her daughters. "We think that it is best for us to move on, girls," she gently suggested. "What do you think?"

Indi grinned. Though she was sorry to hear about her dad's job and stunned that he wouldn't be building houses anymore, she felt like the family already had a plan. They had been dreaming about moving to America for a while, and now that Indi's dad no longer had his job to tie him to India, it was the perfect opportunity.

America would be a new beginning for them. Her smile faded as she realized that it would mean leaving everything here — their house that her dad had designed, her beautiful room, and even her lifelong friends. She felt sure that her dad would build them a new house in America, and with that thought she straightened up.

"We'll have to brush up on the Americans' way of speaking English," Indi commented. She knew that her English would make her stick out like a sore thumb.

Her father smiled and nodded. "We'll hire a tutor for you tomorrow."

"House," the woman patiently remarked. She pointed to the picture in the book and repeated, "House. I live in the house."

"I live in the house," Indi repeated slowly. She glanced up and grinned shyly at the woman — a private American English-speaking tutor her father had hired. "But what if I want to live in a cave?" she asked in her native language.

The woman laughed and shook her head. "I live in the *cave*," she answered. Indi grinned and mimicked her, loving the feel of learning. She was soaking it up like a sponge, and she knew that she had already surpassed her parents' progress. They were pretty stuck in their old ways.

Englan wasn't trying — not really — and before long Indi would be the most fluent of all of them. They had agreed to speak only American English in the house to help everyone adjust more quickly.

"I can't wait to get to America," Indi told her mother as they darted around the kitchen, cooking her father's favorite stew. "It will be an adventure!"

Her mother laughed and nodded, though Indi thought she looked a little sad.

"What's wrong, mother?" she asked tentatively.

Her mother just shook her head and refused to answer. A moment later, the stew boiled over, and Indi was so busy cleaning up the mess that she forgot completely about her mother's sad face.

For the next few weeks, everything was a flurry of activity as they all prepared for the trip to America. Even little Englan helped by packing bedding and clothing into trunks. Indi's dad purchased tickets on one of the highest-rated ocean liners in the world to carry his family to their new homeland. Indi couldn't wait to get started.

Still, there were some difficult days. Indi's friends visited her home almost daily, and one day she finally had to tell them the sad news — she was moving.

"Leaving?" Clem gasped. "Where? Why? When?"

"To America," Indi returned. "We are leaving in a month. I have known for a little while, but I didn't want to tell you guys until it was a definite decision."

"But...but...," Victoria stuttered, her eyes brimming with tears.

Suddenly Indi didn't feel like this was an adventure at all but rather an awful state of affairs. She had known these girls most of her life, had shared everything with them, and now she had to leave them. She could hardly bear the thought.

"I'll write; I really will," she assured them, giving each of them a long hug. "And when I'm older, maybe I can visit you guys."

There were quiet sobs and tears for a while.

Then Olivia straightened up. "Well," she uttered, "you still have a month. I refuse to cry for you now. We'll just have to make sure that this month is a month to remember."

Indi smiled through her own tears and nodded. Olivia was right. If they only had a month left together, they would make it the best month ever — one to remember.

CHAPTER 7

HARD GOODBYES

March 2002

They did have the best month ever, and her friends threw her an intimate farewell party on her last weekend in India. The party was at the lake. They barbequed meat, ate cakes, had balloons, and built another sand castle. Indi headed home afterwards. She was exhausted but certain she had experienced a month she would never forget.

The whole family was sad to leave everything and everyone behind, but they also knew that they were following a calling from God.

"What do you think it will be like?" Indi asked, slipping her hand into her mother's and gazing at the setting sun.

"I'm sure it will be beautiful," her mother answered. "Your father will build us a house just like the one we have here."

"But we'll stay in New York for a while at first to settle in," her father stated, taking Indi's other hand. "Once I obtain some references and a respectable job, we hope to move to the countryside. Perhaps we can buy a farm with many acres so I can build anything that I can dream!"

"And another house like ours? And another little house for Englan and me?" Indi asked wistfully. "And we'll make new friends like the ones we have in India and live happily ever after?"

"Happily ever after, Indi," her parents giggled.

Indi believed them and ran off to finish packing.

The next morning, they packed all their things in boxes, crates, and suitcases. They left their beautiful house. Their furniture wasn't coming with them — it had been sold with the house — but Indi's father assured them that they would purchase upgraded furniture in America. They took their clothes and valuables, her father's designs, and her mother's seamstress supplies. Everything else, Thomas assured them, could be purchased in America.

He shut the front door with a firm grip and slipped the key into the doorknob, turning it once counterclockwise to lock it up for the very last time. Indi swallowed her tears at the idea that this was the last time she would ever lay her beautiful brown eyes on this home. She reached out to lay her fingers on the door one last time.

Then she turned and followed her parents to the waiting taxi.

"Indi, come on!" Englan shouted, bouncing on her toes. "We have to catch the train!"

Indi laughed and quickened her pace, tugging one of her suitcases behind her. When she reached the cab, her suitcase was hoisted up onto the roof. She climbed into her seat and settled in. They were truly on their way now, and though she didn't know what to expect, she couldn't contain the excitement thumping in her heart. The taxicab was only the first part of this fabulous adventure.

Half an hour later, they arrived at the train station, the second part of the journey. After unloading everything and loading it onto the train, they seated and settled themselves comfortably on the train that was headed for Delhi. Indi was happy to have a window seat. She watched as the city that she had always called home grew fainter and farther away.

After the train arrived in Delhi, the family stayed a week with Indi's aunt. They kept busy sightseeing and traveling through the city.

One night, Indi walked into the kitchen to find her parents in a serious discussion with her aunt.

"We're leaving our money with you," her father said. "When we arrive in America, we will send you our contact information so you can wire us the money. We don't want to travel with this much money. We will do well enough without it until we arrive."

"But what if there is an emergency?" her aunt asked nervously. "What if you should need it?"

"Oh, we will be fine," her mother assured her. "This is the best way to keep our money safe."

Indi considered this for a moment and then approached them quietly. "I want to leave some of my money with you as well. Not all of it, of course — there might be a thing I want to buy — but some of it so it's safe."

Indi took out her purse and carefully counted her coins, dividing them in half. The first half she left with her aunt. The second she placed back into her purse.

CHAPTER 8

MORE GOODBYES

The next day, Indi's aunt dropped them off at the Delhi International Airport. It was now time for them to travel to their next destination. Indi hugged her aunt tightly before saying that she loved her very much. Tears streamed down her mother's cheeks as they walked through the terminal, waving goodbye.

The journey to the ship took ages — or so it seemed. They traveled via airplane from Delhi International Airport to Frankfurt Airport in Germany. After they arrived in Germany, there was still more traveling ahead. They traveled on a train to London, passing through the greenest, most lush landscape Indi had ever viewed. In London, they would board the ocean liner that would take them to America. Of course, Indi grabbed the window seat — again.

"It's so different from India," she said, breathing in the sharp scent of trees and soil. Beyond them, the valleys were deep green with vegetation, the mountains bright with their crowns of snow. Even now, in summer, the highest mountains had ice and snow. Indi wondered what it would be like to live there, with cold all year long. In India, they never had snow, and she wondered suddenly if they would have it in America.

She asked, and her mother laughed. "Yes, dear. It will snow every winter in New York, though I don't know if it will snow when we move to the countryside. Look, the steward is here with some dinner for us."

The train steward placed some fresh salads down on the small dining tables next to their seats and walked away.

Indi picked up the fork, but she missed her mouth as she tried to take a bite of her salad because her eyes were still on the grand trees and steep mountainsides. She giggled as she wiped the salad dressing off her cheek. Germany was nothing like India, and she wondered what England would look like.

The next day, they reached London after traveling through a long tunnel that the conductor told her was actually passing under water. Indi didn't like that part of the journey; she felt as if she had to hold her breath. It was a relieving moment when the train exited into the watery lights of England and made its way back onto dry land. Indi ran to the window and gazed behind them, shocked to observe nothing more than a wide expanse of water.

I guess we really were under the ocean and have now safely arrived on the other side as if nothing had ever happened, Indi thought.

Arriving in London at Paddington Station was another shock.

"There are so many people here," Indi whispered. She had never witnessed so many people in one place — and all in such a hurry! *Where could they be headed in such a rush?* Indi wondered.

Her mother giggled. "This is where I grew up, Indi," she answered. "Your father and I are familiar with these kinds of whirlwind crowds."

They headed into the Underground, descending many staircases until they came to a new set of tracks.

"Where are we headed?" Indi inquired nervously.

"We are riding the Underground to the hotel," her father quickly responded. "But do not fret. We are here for two full days, so we will spend plenty of time above ground, sightseeing!"

And view the sights they did indeed. Indi begged to tour Buckingham Palace. For one lump sum price, they were able to visit Windsor Castle, as well. At sunset on the first night, they rode on the London Eye — the largest Ferris wheel Indi had ever laid her eyes on. From the highest part of the ride, all of the London lights could be viewed for miles. It seemed as though Indi could see to the end of the earth.

The next day, they enjoyed a ride on the Duck Tour, which felt familiar — actually, similar to the dragonfly ride Indi had left at home, but this one was under water.

Just when Indi was starting to enjoy the accents of the London people, it was time to board the ship. "How long will we be sailing?" she asked her dad as they began packing their belongings in their cabin.

"Thirteen days," he answered. "There will be stops along the way, of course, because we will pick up new passengers at other ports. Then it's onto the ocean, finally on our way to America!"

Indi and Englan laughed as their excitement about the whole trip grew. They were almost silly and began immediately asking about dinner and dreaming of all the foods they would eat the first night on the ship.

CHAPTER 9

ALL HOPE GONE

The Ship

April 2002

Two days into the journey, life as they knew it began to crumble. It hit her father first. The family was watching dolphins up on the main deck. It was time for bed, so they headed toward their room. That was when it happened. Her father collapsed and fell down several steps to the deck below.

"Dad!" Indi screamed, and she rushed down after him. When she arrived, to her shock she found that he was both hot and sweaty with a fine dew beading on his forehead. His eyes were fluttering, and she couldn't be sure that he was awake or conscious at all.

A moment later, her mother threw herself to the floor next to him. "Thomas!" she yelled, shaking him. She put a hand to his forehead and then another to his neck, and she gasped. "His pulse is weak," she muttered. "Come on, we have to get him to the ship's doctor immediately."

Indi nodded once and grabbed one side of her father, her mother taking his other side. He was barely capable of walking. They half dragged and half pushed him toward the medical bay, where Indi knew nurses were readily available to help those who fell sick during the journey.

Maybe her father had eaten something bad or hadn't had enough sleep the night before. The boat's rocking kept me up most of the night, and perhaps it bothered him as well. Indi's imagination ran away with her thoughts.

They were barely through the door, though, when her mother collapsed as well, gasping and twitching on the floor. Indi shrieked and would have helped her mother, but she was too busy trying to support her father.

"Help!" she cried, looking desperately for the nurses — or anyone! "My parents are sick! Help!"

A woman rushed in from a back room, took one look at Indi and her parents, and immediately called for more help. In a matter of moments, several nurses appeared — and then disappeared with Indi's parents in tow. Indi was left sitting alone in the waiting area.

Before long, another nurse appeared and sat next to her. She cuddled an arm around Indi's shoulders and pulled her in close. "You are a courageous girl for a thirteen-year-old," the nurse observed. "And you did exactly what you needed to do, getting your parents here. They aren't well, though, and I...well, I don't think they'll be returning to your cabin tonight. Are you here alone?"

"Just — just my parents and I," Indi hiccupped. "And my sister, Englan. She's in the play area. We left...we left there so we could — ." Her voice broke. She stopped speaking and began sobbing. *Her parents sick? From what?* Frightened, Indi imagined the worst possible scenario.

"It's okay. Calm down, sweetie. Everything will be alright," the nurse assured her while hugging her close. "Let's pick up your sister together, and then I'll return you to your cabin. It is best for you two to rest well — you might be sick, too."

Later that night, Indi lay in her bed, staring at the ceiling. *How did this happen?*

Not a week earlier, they had been a happy family, excited at the prospect of living in America together and starting a new life. Now…she stifled a sob, not wanting to upset Englan. Her sister was already confused about where their parents were and why they had not returned to their cabin.

Four days passed, and though the girls were doing well enough with the ship-provided food, they had not been allowed to visit or correspond with their parents.

In fact, as they approached the medical bay, the nurses commanded them to leave as it was too dangerous. The girls were immediately returned to their cabin, but not before Indi noticed many worried and sorrowful faces. She was worried sick but tried to hide it from Englan. Something was certainly wrong, and she vowed to get to the bottom of it. She wanted to know what was going on with her parents and when they would be released from the stuffy medical rooms.

Enough was enough! She climbed out of her bed, careful not to wake Englan, and crept to the door, opening it and then shutting it behind her as quietly as she could. Once she was in the hall, she began running. She knew the way to the medical bay by heart now, and it took her little time to get there.

"My parents," she huffed, staring up at the nurse on duty. "I demand to know the whereabouts of my parents. Now!"

The lady's head dropped low, her face full of sympathy. "I'm afraid you cannot speak with your parents. Well, they fell very ill. It was probably from something they contracted while in India. We…we did not have the medicine that they desperately needed to survive, and…well, we did the best we could do with our resources. They…"

"No," Indi uttered in the softest voice because her knees went weak and her voice faded as she suddenly realized what the woman was trying to say. "No. No! NO!" Before she knew it, her voice had risen into a shriek. She boldly darted past the nurse and through the door behind her, casting about, desperately searching for some sign — any sign — of her mom and dad.

They have to be here somewhere; they just have to! She flung herself around one corner and then another, and suddenly she stopped dead in her tracks.

There, on a table in front of her, lay her mother. Breathless. Motionless. More pale than Indi had ever known possible. Her lips faintly tinged blue. On the other side of the table, another body form was covered with a sheet. These were her parents. She did not need to step closer to verify — she knew that they had passed.

CHAPTER 10

A NEW FRIEND

April 2002

"It will give you something to do to take your mind off everything," Joseph, the cruise director, suggested gently. He was staring down into Indi's eyes, obviously very concerned, but Indi could hardly force herself to care.

Her mother and father were gone, and she and her sister were — orphans. She hoped and prayed she would wake up from this nightmare. *My family's broken, and you want me to take my mind off 'things'?!* Indi thought in anger.

Does anyone truly care about us, or are these people just trying to pass the time until they can make us someone else's problem? Indi doubted everyone's intentions.

What would happen to Indi and her sister when they arrived in New York in two days? Where would they stay? What would they do?

She should be worried, she knew, but all she could feel was a deep, dark, hollow place where her heart had been. How could everything have declined so quickly?

Joseph had spent several hours each day with the girls, distracting them and ensuring that they continued to eat and at least stepped into the sunlight. He had been selfless and kind, and although Indi didn't understand his motives, in the end she was very thankful not to be completely alone. She had never before met an adult who was so compassionate and caring, besides her parents, of course.

"Why have you been so nice to us?" Indi inquired softly.

Joseph paused for a moment, shocked by the bold question. Then he answered, "I'm a disciple of Jesus Christ, and I believe in doing unto others as I would have done to myself. If I had children and they landed in your situation, I hope that some kind soul would take care of them. I have watched you two and can project what might become of you without a caregiver. My heart goes out to you, and the Lord has asked me to care for you. I believe He knows best. Do you believe in Jesus?"

Indi tilted her chin, and her teary eyes peered upward. "Yes," she whispered. "I believe He must have brought you to care for us now, when we need you the most."

He nodded wisely and then continued speaking. "I have arranged for both you and your sister to be involved in the production of 'Annie' happening on board the ship. At night, you will return to your cabin to sleep. Food will be provided, of course, but this ... well, it will give you something else to think about."

Indi nodded, too numb to speak, and Joseph left.

Two hours later, she found herself backstage in one of the auditoriums, staring about in confusion. There were so many people, all dressed outlandishly. Her eyes perked up when she noticed the unbelievable props! Even in her home back in India, her eyes had never beheld anything so fanciful. As her eyes moved from one prop to the next, she suddenly noticed a girl, just a little older than herself, standing in the midst of them.

Deciding that she could use a friend about now, she approached the girl. "I'm Indi," she announced, boldly extending her hand.

The girl looked her up and down, her face haughty, until she clearly realized who Indi was. *Had Joseph told everyone?* Indi thought as she shook the girl's hand.

"Ashley's my name. I'm a Hollywood actress. Have you heard of me?"

"No," Indi shook her head. "If you work in Hollywood, what are you doing here?"

"Been doing publicity through Europe for my next movie," the girl quipped. "I agreed to do this play on the way home to keep from being bored. Filming part of my movie on the ship, too." She stopped and looked Indi up and down, then nodded. "Say, we need extras, and you look just the sort. What do you say? You'll earn a little money, and you'll get to be in a movie!"

Indi considered the offer for a moment. Joseph had revealed to her that she was already cast in this play. Did this girl not know that?

"I —," she started, not wanting Ashley to mess up anything if the director had already okayed some deal.

The girl cut her off with a sharp gesture. "Don't worry about it, doll," she commanded. "We'll make sure everything is taken care of. Always do." With that, she turned and strolled away, shouting orders to her right and left.

Indi watched her walk off, confused. Her first impression of Ashley was that she appeared to be decent. She was certainly friendly enough. In fact, she had offered Indi a part in her film, which meant she must have a sharing heart — underneath all of her pretense, that is. Her brash, mouthy attitude delivered the strong impression that she was not an inwardly happy girl, though. Not *truly* happy.

Personally, Indi believed that Ashley was a girl who needed to find the joy of the Lord — you only had to look into her eyes to know that she didn't have Him!

As it turned out, Indi spent much more time with Ashley than she had expected. When she went to the set the next morning as instructed by Joseph, she found Ashley sitting by herself on the deck, an impromptu picnic spread out before her.

"Sit!" Ashley mumbled around a mouth full of food. "I didn't have time for breakfast this morning, so they brought this out here for me. Want some eggs? Toast?"

Indi shook her head but sat willingly. "I had breakfast with my sister, but thanks."

Ashley looked up. "Just your sis — ?" She broke off and pressed her lips together, and her eyes grew wide. "Oh. Right. I forgot." She breathed a deep, shaky breath and squinted her eyes a little bit. Indi saw a tear but assumed it was probably her imagination. Ashley didn't seem like the super-sentimental type. What could this girl possibly be crying about? From what Indi had heard, Ashley had everything a girl her age could ever dream of.

"I'm sorry about your parents," Ashley said, hanging her head. "I lost someone once, and I know…well, I know how it feels."

Indi stared at her, shocked. Of all the things she had imagined could come from Ashley's mouth, that had *not* ever been an option! For a moment, Indi thought she might have found a real friend — a girl she could actually talk to.

As suddenly as the moment happened, it was over. Ashley's eyes shot to something beyond Indi. She jumped to her feet, calling out to someone.

"Eat whatever you want, doll! I've had enough," she yelled back at Indi. "I got to run to the set. See ya." She strutted off, leaving Indi confused and somehow saddened. She thought that Ashley had everything a girl could want. Now she realized the girl was not only unhappy but also lonely, and she was hiding it all behind the person she pretended to be.

CHAPTER 11

THE SHIP DOCKED

April 2002

Finally, after thirteen tragic days of Indi sharing time between their cabin, the dining room, and the movie set, the long, windy, and cold ride was over, and they had officially arrived in America. The idea of being alone in a new country terrified Indi; she had been counting on her parents to take care of them and guide them into the country and tell them what to do, to ensure that they would be safe.

She gazed out over the water to where the Statue of Liberty proudly held her torch over the bay of New York and beyond, to where the city's buildings stretched their fingers up to the sky.

What are we supposed to do now? Indi trembled.

Then, as if in answer to her internal question, Joseph appeared at her side. "I know this may not be what you want to hear right now, but I grew up in the United States. I know of a kind Christian couple in

Oklahoma — they run an orphanage. I would be honored to escort you there. It is the nicest orphanage around, and they can help you find a permanent family."

Indi gasped in shock. She was having enough trouble with the idea that her parents would never return to hold her again, the idea of never again spotting glimpses of her mother's smiling face or hearing the vision of her father's next home to build. The ramifications were too intensely painful to consider. She had been avoiding reflecting on the what-ifs for as long as she could.

Now she and her sister would have to face the facts. Their parents were gone. They had no other choice but to allow Joseph to assist them to the orphanage.

People who are not able to have children on their own will probably come stare at us like we are now for sale. Indi imagined the worst-case scenario. *We will be like zoo animals on display.* Oh, it pained her to consider joining another family. *Perhaps we wouldn't be able to stay together. Stop imaging all these awful future outcomes, Indi.* She straightened up her inward thoughts.

She sucked in a breath and then suddenly remembered something. "No, we still have family — an aunt, in Delhi. She is holding our money, in fact. I will call her. Surely she will send for us and rescue us from this nightmare."

She looked up at the man, tears stinging the corners of her eyes.

He frowned and then nodded. "I will take you to the office in port so you can use the telephone." He laid a gentle hand on her shoulder, as if that would comfort her. "Call your aunt to see if she can help you."

Indi nodded back, praying that at least their aunt would fly them home. This was their one chance to try to stitch their lives back together again — but they would still never be the same.

CHAPTER 12

ORPHANED

April 2002

"Your mother and father, dead?" her aunt gasped. "How? When?"

"The nurse said it was something they had contracted in India," Indi answered, trying hard to hold back the tears dying to pour out of her eyes. Saying it aloud like this — telling her aunt what had happened — made it feel more real, and her heart squeezed at the thought. "Please, Aunt Loraine, I know they left money with you. Please arrange for us to come home to live with you! Otherwise..." Her voice faded off.

There was a long, heavy silence on the other end of the line, and Indi held her breath. What was taking so long? What delayed her response?

Finally, the woman cleared her throat and responded, "I'm afraid I cannot do that, Indi, dear. I thought I was doing the right thing, but..."

She continued on, explaining each detail, and every word sank like a dagger into Indi's heart. By the time she hung up the phone, Indi felt as if her entire world — what was left of it — had shattered.

"What did she say?" Joseph asked anxiously. "Is she sending money? Plane tickets?"

Indi gazed at him, then turned to her sister. "Indi?" Englan asked, confused and afraid since she knew by the look on Indi's face that the call did not turn out as expected.

Indi closed her eyes and pondered deeply the next step. *How am I supposed to tell them what I just heard? How can I break Englan's heart the way mine was just broken?*

She finally opened her mouth, unsure of what she meant to say, and let the words flow out in a rush. "Aunt Loraine doesn't have the money anymore, so she is no help to us."

"What?" Joseph gasped.

"She invested it. She believed it was a solid investment. She assumed she would earn more money and be able to surprise my parents with the profits. The company she invested in failed. She lost every dollar and does not have the finances to bring us home."

Another long, sad pause followed her words, and then the man pulled her and Englan roughly toward him, holding them closely as all three sobbed and sobbed.

Sometime later, he murmured, "I'm so sorry. I will escort you to the orphanage. They will provide a nice home for now."

Indi plugged her ears — not with her fingers, of course; that would be rude. She did not want to listen. She didn't want to hear that she was out of options.

She glanced down at her sister, who looked up with large, tearful eyes and gave one sorrowful nod. Indi nodded back. They just knew.

They knew what the other sister was feeling. No one else could understand the hurt.

"Okay," she whispered. "We will pack our things." She took her sister's hand and turned back toward their cabin, trying to straighten her spine. Whatever happened, they were in it together, and as the older sister she needed to be as strong as she could be. She would be as strong as her friend Clem and even stronger.

As soon as they exited the boat, being able further to deny their situation was ridiculously impossible.

Joseph watched the girls walk back toward their cabin; his heart broke into a million pieces at the sight. He knew their pain all too well. He had walked in their shoes before — he had lost his mother just recently, and though he was middle-aged and had spent so many years with her, the loss had still crushed him. There really is never a good time to lose someone you love.

He couldn't imagine dealing with such a loss as a child, and in such a terrible way, *while* also losing a father.

Indi was doing an admirable job of holding herself together, but he did not know how much longer she would be able to continue. He needed to get them to a safe haven quickly so that healing could begin.

The orphanage will be the perfect place. He just knew it.

CHAPTER 13

THE FIRST MEETING

"Why, Joseph!" a voice suddenly cried out, and Joseph whirled around, wondering who had found him. To his surprise, he saw Jack and Alyssa, Ashley's parents.

"Jack, Alyssa!" he greeted them, striding toward them with his hand outstretched and a grin on his face. Although he had trouble with Ashley on set, he had known her parents for many years. They had mutual admiration and respect for one another.

"How are you?" Alyssa asked, smiling. "We decided to come ourselves to pick up Ashley. Have you seen her?"

"I believe she is still packing her things. Her agent's with her, of course, but they were filming until late last night, so they didn't have a chance to pack. Any moment they will be arriving. It is wonderful that you two are personally here to pick her up!"

Jack paused and slid his eyes toward Alyssa, who glanced at him once and nodded with approval. "Well, we wanted to talk to you about something, actually. We've decided that Ashley's been an only child for long enough. We are too old to have any children of our own, of course, but the girl…well, she has become a bit spoiled. We know she is lonely."

Joseph nodded. He had noticed it also but believed it wasn't his place to bring it to their attention.

"We think she needs a sister. Perhaps two," Alyssa added, winking. "What do you think?"

Joseph paused. He was stunned really. Were they implying what he thought they were? His heart pounded with excitement! *A home for the girls — already?* he thought. It was all he could do to refrain from a celebratory dance!

Oh, but how would Ashley respond to this news? He just didn't know how Ashley would react to it. "I agree that Ashley could use a companion, but after the…well…" He let his voice drift off, deliberately attempting not to revisit the painful subject of their family's loss.

"Is it maybe a bit too soon for Ashley — for you?" he asked respectfully. "It has only been a year since…Perhaps you should process the gravity of this decision some more before we amp up the girl's hope for a family. Maybe you could spend some quality time with Ashley first to see where her heart is these days. I know she has missed you," Joseph urged them.

Suddenly he felt a delicate hand threading its way through his fist, and he turned. To his surprise, he saw Indi and Englan standing next to him, their eyes large and frightened. Englan had her hand in his, and he squeezed it, then turned back to Jack and Alyssa.

"Jack, Alyssa, this is Indi and Englan. They…well, sadly they lost their parents just days ago on this trip to America. I have had the joy of taking them under my wing, so to speak. I am their guardian angel…for now anyway." He squeezed the girl's hand in love. "I plan to find them a home in Oklahoma, at Jenny's Home — it's an orphanage. It is just temporary until God places them into a new loving family."

Jack and Alyssa both gasped in horror — as they had known such a painful loss as this. Alyssa dropped to her knees. "Oh, you poor dears," she blundered through tears as she wrapped the girls tightly in her arms. "Oh, you poor darlings, I'm so sorry."

Englan fell into the woman's arms, taking full advantage of a mother figure, while Indi lifted her chin and stepped back. "Thank you, ma'am. We're…we just want to get away from this awful ship and all the terrible memories that are here."

The woman nodded and then looked up at Joseph. "Well, go then, but please let us know if there's anything we can do for you."

Joseph nodded, filing their offer away in the back of his mind. Right now there was nothing more he could do for the girls, but in the future there might be.

CHAPTER 14

OKLAHOMA

April 2002

After the ship docked, Joseph returned to their cabin to find them clinging to one another. He took their hands. "I have already purchased your tickets for Oklahoma City. My longtime friends know about your arrival and are preparing a place for you right now. You will be comfortable, at least until you find your way forward."

Joseph personally knew the owners of the orphanage. He would accompany Indi and Englan to ensure their safe arrival. He led Indi and Englan off the ship and away from the last place they would ever see their parents. They slid into a cab with their parcels and rode to the train station. The belongings her parents had shipped ahead would unfortunately have to be sold to pay for their expenses.

The station was even *more* crowded and terrifying than the one at Paddington. Joseph herded Indi and Englan into the seats of a clean personal compartment.

"We will arrive in Oklahoma within one day," he said kindly. "I would suggest that you two sleep now, while you can. Once we arrive, there will be much scurrying about — you will need your rest."

CHAPTER 15

THE ARRIVAL

Oklahoma

May 2002

Indi gasped and jumped out of her sleep, her heart racing. It had been THAT dream again — the dream where her parents had died and she and Englan were left alone. She glanced about, expecting to see the cabin of their ship, and tried to sort her thoughts, but the room around her was unfamiliar, and she could feel beneath her not the slow, rolling rock of a ship but a sharp, jerky motion. One swift turn and then another. She scowled.

Then every detail of the past two weeks came rushing back into her mind. Not the ship. This was not the ship at all, and it hadn't been a dream. Not at all! Her mind screamed with panic. Her parents were gone. Now she and Englan were on their way to an orphanage — run by people they were clueless about — in a foreign land! Indi felt sweaty chills run down her spine.

Across from her, Englan was sleeping with her head leaned up against Joseph's shoulder. Indi envied her the soft, innocent look on her face. She turned toward the window and saw that the train was, in fact, slowing down. They were coming to their first and only stop: the town in Oklahoma that housed the orphanage.

Once the train had come to a stop, Joseph and Englan were awake.

Indi gazed at the building outside of her window, thinking immediately that it was at least nicer than the house where Clem lived. The paint was a bright, cheerful blue; the shutters were blindingly white; and the roof was made of muted red shingles. She saw a face pressed against a window — and then two faces — and out of the corner of her eye caught the flash of another child running past an open doorway.

"So this will be our home until we're old enough to leave this place," she sarcastically murmured under her breath so that no one could hear.

"Or until you get adopted." Joseph had heard Indi's discouraged comment. "You must remain hopeful, Indi. Many couples cannot have children of their own and search to find children just like you to love. I pray that you and Englan will have new parents soon and a house to call your own."

Indi looked away from Joseph up to the house in front of her and wondered. *After all that has happened, I am just not sure I can ever have hope again.*

CHAPTER 16

BIRTHDAY CELEBRATION

January 2003

Indi stifled her giggles, trying desperately to stir the cake batter without spilling any. She was in a rush because she had overslept — shocking, considering how closely the orphanage monitored their schedules — so she didn't get the cake started as early as she had wanted. Now there were only two hours before the party, which meant it would have to be a regular birthday cake rather than individual cupcakes like Englan had requested this year. A regular cake would bake faster and would be easier to ice.

They had already lived in the orphanage for over six months now, and Indi was happier than she could ever have imagined. Still, every single night she had recurring nightmares about losing her parents. She missed her mother and father desperately, but she and Englan had formed a new family.

The couple who owned the orphanage ensured that the children received an education, meals, and warm beds. There were enough girls their age that both Indi and Englan had made a number of close new friendships. Best of all, the owners were Christians, and Indi and Englan were being raised in the faith their parents had previously rooted them in.

And now Englan was about to have her seventh birthday. Birthdays at the orphanage were the best days of the year for the kids. On those days, none of the orphans had to do anything — they enjoyed pure freedom from, well, everything! No chores, no school, no work. Just fun, fun, and more fun! The birthday boy or girl was treated like royalty. On the girls' birthdays, the orphanage was decorated like a palace, and a massive tea party was always in full swing in the fondly named "Royal Party Room." Englan was, of course, excited about her birthday, especially about the palace theme, which reminded her of her room in India.

With the skills her mother had taught her, Indi had sewn Englan a special birthday gown for this birthday event — to help take Englan's mind off the fact that their parents would not be present. Many of their new friends pitched in a helping hand to put together this royal ball, tea party, and dinner. There was also the promise of late-night movies in the living room. It would be the most special birthday ever!

As Indi stirred the cake batter, she grinned again. She couldn't help but be excited for Englan's birthday. Still, there was something bittersweet about it. This was Englan's first birthday that her parents would miss, and this celebration would be quite different from the ones they had had at home. In fact, living in America was considerably different from what their life in India had been.

Overall, Indi really did not mind living at the orphanage. Her favorite thing was working with the cook, who was teaching her how to bake her favorite dishes.

The cook had become one of Indi's favorite people. They often played jokes on one another. One time, Indi had baked a ring from a gumball machine into a loaf of bread and made sure the cook got that piece. Another time, the cook had put chili seasoning in with some cinnamon on Indi's toast. Indi was not exactly thrilled with that one. She probably drank a gallon of water that day. Indi's favorite joke was on her birthday, when the cook had acted like she had no idea what day it was. Indi was a little bit disappointed, but then the cook had gathered everyone in the lunchroom for a surprise — a magician, who had performed just for Indi's birthday.

Of course, the practical jokes they played on one another only made them closer. To Indi, the cook was the most important person at the orphanage next to Englan, who didn't count because she was far too young *really* to talk to about anything. Although she didn't have her parents anymore, she knew that she was blessed to have friends and someone like the cook.

She went back to mixing, stirring furiously to get the lumps out of the cake batter. What was she doing daydreaming when she had so much baking to do? This was a day for celebration, not a day to live in the past with regrets.

CHAPTER 17

CHOSEN

Hollywood

March 2003

"She needs a friend, Alyssa, someone who will be there for her when she wants to talk. Someone who can remind her how to be a child," Jack tried to convince his wife. They had been watching Ashley on the set of one of her movies and had already agreed that she was not well — not sick, just not whole.

Alyssa nodded, just as concerned as her husband. Ashley did indeed need something else: a good friend who would impact her life in a more positive direction. They brainstormed ideas of people they knew and concluded that a good Christian girl would have the right kind of influence with Ashley. They stopped to pray for God to direct them to a solution.

Suddenly, God reminded Alyssa of a person perfect for Ashley and their family! She spun toward her husband, excitedly taking his hands. "Those girls! Those girls," she spluttered. "The orphaned girls on the cruise ship. Joseph took them to a home after their parents died on the ship."

Jack held his hands up, laughing. "Slow down! What girls? What are you talking about? Joseph?"

Alyssa laughed, barely able to contain her enthusiasm. "Yes! The girls, remember the girls on the cruise ship when we picked up Ashley last spring? They were good girls — they must have been, or Joseph wouldn't have been so attached to them! Don't you agree...do you think...perhaps?"

Jack's face cleared then, and Alyssa could practically see the wheels turning in his mind. "I'll call him this afternoon," he promised. "I *do* believe...yes. It would be perfect."

Joseph couldn't believe it. "Of course!" he cried, overjoyed at the suggestion. This time, he knew the timing was perfect. "I'm happy to help! I know Ashley has to be a good Christian girl under that hard Hollywood actress she pretends to be. Let me make a few calls."

Joseph knew the moment he hung up the phone what to do. He made one more call — directly to the orphanage owners.

"Are Indi and Englan, the two girls from India, still there?" he asked breathlessly, praying that they hadn't been adopted yet. He couldn't imagine any girls more suitable for this particular family, and he knew that Ashley's parents would love and cherish the two girls he loved and had supported so much on the cruise ship.

When the owner responded with a "YES" that the two girls were still living with them, he jumped for joy.

"I'm coming to get them," he quickly responded. "Please have them ready for me in one week. I've found a home for them."

He hung up the phone, took a deep breath, and then called Ashley's parents. "I have requested the adoption of Indi and Englan, the two girls you suggested. It's been over six months since you all met, and before I take them from their home now, I need to verify that you are absolutely positive you will provide them with a new home and family!"

There was a long, heavy pause on the other end of the line, and Joseph cringed. What if they changed their minds? He would have to call the orphanage back and tell them that the girls weren't wanted anymore.

Before Jack spoke, he cleared his throat, and it sounded to Joseph like he had been fighting back tears. "That sounds absolutely perfect. We were already confident before we contacted you. We hope and pray that they will be able to easily accept our family as their family. Two girls are even better than one, and Indi is the same age as Ashley — "

"And they've already met!" Alyssa interrupted. "They've already met, and Ashley offered her work — "

"That's exactly why I love that you asked for them!" Joseph joyfully replied. "They already got along so well; it would be perfect!" The three adults laughed, quite pleased with themselves, and then proceeded to make their plans.

CHAPTER 18

THE PICKUP

Oklahoma

One Week Later

Jack and Alyssa met Joseph at the airport in Oklahoma City, Oklahoma, their bags in hand.

"Are you ready?" Joseph asked in anticipation. He was beyond thrilled at the prospect of hugging the girls he had grown to love over those two weeks! "I called Jenny, so she knows we are on our way. She hasn't said anything to Indi or Englan about our plans yet. In fact, she arranged a luncheon so that you can see the girls without them knowing you are there for them."

Jack ducked down and picked up Alyssa's bag, his expression intent. "Perfect. We won't change our minds, I'm sure, but this way we can see how they get along at the orphanage. Let's move onward." The three of them turned and walked quickly toward the exit.

When they arrived at the orphanage, they found that the dining room was set up with several long tables and chairs and decorated with streamers and balloons. Jenny had also invited several other couples, who gathered with Alyssa, Jack, and Joseph in the main foyer, talking quietly amongst themselves about whom they hoped to find and adopt.

"They told the children that it is only a party," Joseph said, having asked Jenny what was going on. "It's a special lunch so that they can meet some of the people who help to pay for the orphanage."

Alyssa frowned. "The kids don't know that these people might adopt them?"

He shook his head. "Certainly not. Telling them that these people might take someone home would only get their hopes up, and what if the couples didn't choose any children for their own? You can see how that would just lead to possibly devastating disappointment."

Jack nodded, his face thoughtful. "So Indi and Englan don't know that we are here for them. They don't know that *you're* here. Do you think they will recognize us?"

Joseph shrugged. "I have no idea. I was only present for a moment during an extremely upsetting time. I have no idea whether they will remember me. Englan, probably not. I don't believe she spoke more than two words to me over those two weeks."

"But you're certain that they are still here," Alyssa confirmed. "And you believe they are right for our family?"

"Oh, yes," Joseph answered quickly. He had never doubted it, and he let that be known. He turned to the sound of Jenny opening the doors of the dining room.

"Ladies and gentlemen, we are ready," she announced. "Please come in and seat yourselves. The children will be here in a few moments."

Indi glanced around the room, surprised, and reached down to take Englan's hand. "Why are we having a party?" Englan leaned up and over to whisper into Indi's ear.

"I don't know," Indi whispered back, shaking her head. "Jenny only said that she prepared a special luncheon for us. Look, there are visitors here." She pointed toward the far side of the room, where she could see several adults. Her eyes scanned the unfamiliar people, and she wondered why they were here.

"All grown-ups," Englan observed, as if Indi could not see that for herself. "Who are they, Indi?"

Indi paused for a long moment, trying hard to remember Jenny's words exactly. *People who helped to fund the orphanage.* But as she watched, she sensed that more was going on. As the children filed in, husbands and wives evaluated each one closely, pointing at some and leaning in toward each other. Whispering. Nodding and smiling.

They weren't investors at all, she realized. They were there to consider adopting some of the children.

"Those are *parents*," she whispered, pulling Englan closer to her.

"What?" Englan asked, surprised.

"They're couples — parents who are pointing at us and...probably deciding whether they like us — for possible adoption!" Suddenly the excitement Indi had felt at the thought of a party drained away.

They were here to choose children of their own. This was the first time she had witnessed such a thing. It both terrified and excited her. Her mind began to race. Parents. New families. People who wanted children and could take them away from this place.

She dearly loved Jenny and her husband, and she appreciated

everything they had done for Englan and her, but oh how she longed to be part of a family again!

One of those couples might…But what if they don't like me? Worse, what if they want me but not Englan? Or vice versa — they take Englan but not me? Her hand clamped involuntarily on Englan's at the thought. Worst-case scenarios ran through Indi's brain like a speeding train. It was as if every emotion possible pulsed through her body.

Englan squirmed. "Indi, you're hurting me! Let go, let go!" She shook her hand, but Indi refused to release it. No, she would never let Englan go without her. She would never go anywhere without Englan. They were sisters, and the only family they had left.

At that thought, Indi leaned down toward Englan and finally dropped to her knees in front of her sister. "Englan, tell me something," she urged, her voice low and rushed. "Promise me that no matter what happens, you won't ever leave me. Tell me that we're a team and that we will always stick together."

Englan paused, her eyes growing wide and fearful, and then threw her arms around her older sister. "Of course we're a team, Indi," she promised. "I would never go anywhere without you. You're my sister."

Indi breathed a sigh of relief and then glanced to the side to see a pair of large brown loafers standing next to her.

"Well, I must admit, I didn't think I would see you two again," a familiar voice sounded in Indi's ears. "You girls are a sight for sore eyes!"

Indi looked up, confused, and saw a man she had thought she would never lay her eyes on again. "Joseph!" she cried, and she began sobbing uncontrollably.

Joseph folded both girls into his arms.

"You're here!" She threw her arms around him. Even though he was present for some of the saddest days of her life, Indi was thankful that he had found them again. "How are you? Where have you been?" Although the man had only made a brief appearance in their lives, he had become one of their dearest friends because he was there when they needed him most. She was overjoyed to see him again.

Joseph chuckled, then disentangled her arms from around his waist and pushed her gently back. "Indi, it's good to see you. And you, too, Englan," he added, nodding to the younger girl. Then he stooped down in front of Indi, his face carefully blank. "I have brought you a surprise. Are you ready for it?"

"Are you ready to meet them?" he clarified.

Meet whom? Indi wondered, her heart pounding out of her chest. *Did Joseph want to adopt us? Did he find us a family? I'm scared, nervous. I hope I don't wake up if this is a dream.*

The orphanage owners stepped into the reunion. "Indi, Englan, Joseph brought a family that is interested in meeting you. Would you like to meet them?"

Indi paused for a long time before she replied, "They want us? Both of us?"

The woman nodded, smiling. "Yes, and they are waiting for you both in the living room. They requested you specifically, and Joseph agreed that you two would be a perfect fit in their family. They're ready to take you home — if you are willing. Also, you already know their daughter."

Indi raised her eyebrows. "I do?"

The man smiled as well. "We were told that you acted with their only daughter on the cruise ship. Evidently, she gave you a role in her movie."

Indi frowned, thinking, *A girl who gave me a role?* She remembered acting in the play on the ship, but she had worked diligently to forget everything about the ship journey and was having trouble remembering any details. After losing her parents, she had been in such a fog that she could barely function.

She and Englan visited over an hour with Joseph and his friends, Jack and Alyssa, asking and answering questions so they could get to know each other again. Indi had yet to make the connection that Jack and Alyssa were Ashley's parents. This couple wanted to adopt both Englan and Indi, and that was enough for her!

Besides, she fell in love with them immediately.

She found herself grinning, despite her nerves. "Well, I guess we should start packing then, shouldn't we?" she confirmed.

The couple laughed and nodded. Indi and Englan ran off to prepare their things and deliver the news to the other girls.

CHAPTER 19

DEPARTURE

March 2003

"So we're really moving to Hollywood?" Indi asked, watching out the orphanage window for the taxicab's arrival. "And Joseph, can we visit you often?"

"Yes and yes," he laughed. "Jack and Alyssa are lifelong friends of mine, and I'm sure we'll be able to visit each other as often as we would like."

At that, Indi walked over to Jack and Alyssa — her new mom and dad (she almost had to pinch herself to make sure she wasn't dreaming) — and smiled shyly. She wasn't sure why they had chosen her or what they would expect, but the thought of a new family and a real home was almost too marvelous to bear. It was a sharp, bright thought that brought with it both extreme sorrow and pain. The last time she had had a home, it was in India with her parents, whom she missed terribly.

Now it was time to move forward with their lives. She knew that both her mother and father would have wanted that. It had been her responsibility to care for Englan, and now she would have a mother to help her. Her excitement began to grow.

She grinned at Jack and Alyssa and then laughed aloud at the sudden twist her life had taken. Alyssa took Indi's hand and then Englan's as the cab pulled up to the steps of the orphanage. Brimming with joy, the three of them skipped through the crowd of kids, shouting their final goodbyes as they hopped into the taxi waiting at the curb.

They traveled to a nearby airport because Oklahoma was a long way from California. An airplane is much quicker transportation than a train. Jack had purchased first-class tickets for the whole family.

Indi climbed into her seat on the airplane.

She had never before laid eyes on anything so luxurious. The chair was wide, long, and comfy enough for her to lie down. It even spun around, so she could annoy other passengers when she became bored. Next to her, Englan was already busy trying to master the headphones. Joseph had made himself right at home, ordering drinks and food for the three of them. Jack and Alyssa were nestled in the row behind them, so Indi could turn and glance at them through the seat crack. Alyssa managed to spot her every time she did and responded with a bright, cheerful smile.

Jack, on the other hand, responded with one wink — then another. Then he must have worn himself out because he put on an eye mask and leaned his chair back to rest.

Alyssa shot him one disgusted look and then rolled her eyes in Indi's direction. "He claims that he gets sick on planes unless he sleeps," she said in a sassy whisper. "He probably won't wake up until we land. However, if you feel like talking, just come share my seat with me!"

Indi agreed, then took a deep breath and turned to gaze out the airplane window. She had been content at the orphanage, or at least as happy as she could be, but now they were starting on a new adventure.

She was very tired of not having a real home — a mom to hold her when she was sad and a daddy's lap to sit in (she really missed cuddles with her dad). If this couple could offer them a permanent place to call their own, plus comfort and love, then she knew she would happily love them forever.

The moment Indi walked off the plane, she remembered the girl who had granted her a role in her movie and paid her a meager wage merely to stand in the background. She wouldn't have remembered, of course, if it had only been up to her, but that very same girl was standing there in the greeting area, scowling at her, and that jogged her memory.

"I know you from somewhere," Ashley greeted her, frowning. "Where do I know you from? Have we ever acted together?"

"Yes, on a cruise ship once," Indi answered in her soft voice. She believed it would be a welcome realization, but to Indi's surprise, it made Ashley scowl even more. Things escalated when they arrived at their new home and were quickly informed that their room was not yet ready.

"The three of you will be bunking together for a few days just like real sisters — won't that be fun? It will be like a slumber party!" Alyssa exclaimed.

Indi grinned; she had already decided that she liked Alyssa and Jack very much — they were kindhearted and cheerful and had warmly welcomed Englan and Indi. Ashley, however, appeared less than pleased.

"I've never shared a room with anyone — why should I start now?" she pouted.

Indi frowned. Perhaps this would not turn out as well as she had anticipated.

CHAPTER 20

NEW ROOM

April 2003

After a month of sleeping on blow-up beds in Ashley's room, trying to avoid her tantrums as much as they could, Indi and Englan learned that their room was finally ready.

"Thank God," Indi said quietly when she heard the news. "I don't think I could stand another night in Ashley's room."

"Indi!" Englan scolded. "Be nice. She doesn't know how to be kind. It's our job to teach her."

Indi made a sassy face at her little sister, but she knew that Englan was right.

Ashley was the most spoiled girl in the universe, according to Indi's opinion. She could be downright mean. She had barely spoken to them in the month since they had come to live with her. She was away at work on most days anyhow, but she never invited them to join her and never spent time with them when she was at home.

Indi and Englan had been left on their own to explore the house and the neighborhood around it. Jack and Alyssa accompanied them when they left the boundary of their street, but Ashley never offered to join them. Indi didn't think she was actually a bad girl. She was just a girl with no friends, a girl who didn't understand how to be kind. She had never had to practice kindness before now.

Indi believed that something deeper was the source of Ashley's attitude — something that no one had shared with her yet. She had heard pieces of conversations and seen tears in Ashley's eyes more than once…all things that made her conclude there was more to her story than she realized.

Perhaps Ashley really *did* need a close friend.

When they walked into their newly finished room, all thoughts of Ashley flew out of Indi's mind. "Woah!"

Their bedroom, which was next door to Ashley's, was huge. It had its very own private bathroom. Beds lined both walls. She could walk into the closet. Dressers filled two corners of the room. An enormous hammock littered with brightly colored stuffed animals and pillows hung in another corner. Someone — perhaps Alyssa — had painted the one free wall with rainbows and flowers. Their boxes had been moved down from the attic — all their things and even some of the things that had belonged to their parents.

"How did they know we would treasure these things?" Indi asked, fingering one of her mother's bolts of cloth. "How did they get it?"

"It was your friend Joseph's idea," Alyssa responded from the doorway. She had been listening in on the girls. "He bought some of it when they unloaded it from the ship. He thought you would love to have it."

Indi looked at Alyssa with tears streaming from her eyes and thanked God for the second chance she and her sister had been given and for the family and friends they had already made. She missed her parents terribly, but she and Englan had a new family now, and these people were already proving how much they cared.

One day, Alyssa decided to take Indi and Englan to the set with Ashley so they could see how a movie was made. The set was a strange new world for Indi, full of wires, cameras, scaffolding, and background props — a world that she assumed was the set of a European street. Ashley and her co-star were acting as kids who were lost in Paris, trying to find their way home. Indi was told that these two characters had fallen in love in the movie, and the stars were shooting some love scenes that Alyssa did *not* appreciate. Indi watched one scene being shot, and she could see why. She realized immediately why Ashley behaved the way she did. She didn't know Jesus. Indi began to realize that maybe this was her purpose, that God had called her to Hollywood for just this reason: to help Ashley see how much God loved her!

"Englan," Indi said, pulling her sister aside, "we have to talk to Ashley about Jesus. Look, she doesn't know Him, and this void is what has made her angry and bitter. I bet if we talk to her about Him, it will change everything. I mean everything!"

Englan made a doubting face. "I don't think anything could make her *change*, Indi. She's impossible," she said wryly.

"Maybe not," Indi answered, "but we have to at least try."

Englan took a long look at her big sister, then shrugged, putting on the sideways grin that their father had always loved. "If you say so, sis, but don't blame me if it doesn't work!"

CHAPTER 21

THE TRUTH COMES OUT

April 2003

After dinner, Indi and Englan filed into Ashley's room and found her on her bed, painting her nails.

"Well, if it isn't the terrible twosome," she snapped. "What do you two want?"

Indi took a deep breath and quickly decided to jump right in without being put off by Ashley's attitude. "We want to talk to you about Jesus. I've seen how unhappy you are, and there is a real hope for you that can turn it all around. There's something more substantial than us, more important than us."

"Are you kidding me? You sound just like my parents," Ashley responded angrily. "I don't want to hear it from them, and I certainly don't want to hear it from the likes of you."

She paused. Indi and Englan remained silent because they were not sure how to react.

"I'll tell you what," Ashley offered in a softened tone, "I *did* believe in Jesus once — years ago — until the tragedy happened.

"We went to church every Sunday. We were such an intricate part of that church family that we even donated toward the renovation. My sister and I were so excited. The old wooden pews were replaced with soft, red-velvet, cushioned ones. They built a new, gigantic stage so the two of us could perform together in the Easter cantata and present special songs throughout the year. We were two peas in pod — that's what everyone called us.

"We watched from that stage as they hung the most beautiful crystal chandelier. It was gold-trimmed and exactly what I imagined we might see in heaven someday. It was the most beautiful church in California. Then one Sunday, after the preacher began his sermon proclaiming that there was nothing greater than the Lord, the ground began to shake — it was an earthquake.

When it stopped, we thought everything was fine, but my sister, in fear, had bolted out of the pew. That was when it happened. Above my sister's head was the beautiful, heavenly, three-hundred-pound chandelier. It knocked loose and came crashing down and landed on my sister! The noise was a sound I care never to hear again. It crushed her frail body. My sister was killed at church, and my whole world fell apart.

Up until last year, I struggled daily to overcome the pain of losing my sister. I replayed the scene over and over again in my mind. I missed my sister desperately. Some days, it didn't feel real. Other days, I would have rather stayed in my bed all day than do anything else. I was pitiful, sad, lonely, and hurting.

"My mom forced me to audition for a role in a movie. I got a little part. That's when I found something to live for again. My mom pushed me more and more so that I would choose to live again — even if it was without my sister. I needed this drastic change to help the memories of that awful day to grow dim.

"Still, the day that it happened, I decided that I would never trust God again. I promised myself that I would never become a follower of Christ. How could I? Not after what God did to my sister! Never. I will never change my mind for my parents' sake, and I will certainly not change it for you."

Indi, with tears streaming down her cheeks because she knew the pain of losing her parents, paused at this terrible story. The pieces suddenly began falling into place. She recounted the conversations she had overheard since her arrival. The truth was out now. She had always discerned that something inside of Ashley was broken. Now she understood the source of all that anger and pain.

The tears that had flooded Ashley's eyes on the cruise ship when she had shared about losing someone close and important to her suddenly made sense. Indi reached out and laid her hand on Ashley's arm. "That's terrible," she whispered. "Do you want to talk about it? You were there for me when my parents died. If you need me…"

Ashley shrugged off Indi's hand. "It's not like you can change it. It was a long time ago. You can't help. The only way you could help is if you could make it *un*-happen, and you certainly can't do that!"

"But if you want to talk about it …," Englan murmured, moving forward to stand closer to the older girls.

Ashley looked up. Indi could see tears on her eyelashes. "She was my best friend. We did everything together, just like the two of you. And then suddenly she was gone. I don't…I don't think I have ever been happy a single day since I lost her. I miss her so much."

Indi pulled their new sister into her arms, heartbroken. "I know," she said softly. "I felt the same way when my parents died, and no matter how much I love Alyssa and Jack, I don't think it will ever fade. If we didn't still miss them, wouldn't that mean that we had forgotten how much we loved them?" They cried and cried in each other's arms.

Then Indi finally broke the silence. "The Bible tells us that God did not kill your sister. The Lord has many names, but murderer isn't one of them. He is the life giver."

Ashley snorted. "You don't know anything about the real world or how to survive in it."

"My mom and dad both died within days of each other on that ship where I met you," she said sharply. "I DO know about the real world and how terrible things can happen even to good people. Now, can you get any more real than that? Yet I still believe God doesn't cause those bad things to happen. It's the enemy who is in this world to steal, kill, and destroy. Jesus is life, Ashley! You're on the wide path with everyone who believes that you have to tear others down and walk all over them to get what you want so you can be happy, but that path leads to destruction — destruction of families, friendships, and so much more. The narrow path — the one that is in Jesus — is where you need to be!"

Indi paused, breathing heavily, and watched Ashley closely. Her face seemed to be gentler than it ever had been before, but she still had that stubborn slant to her jaw, like she wasn't buying what Indi was pitching.

Englan ignored all of Ashley's stubborn body language and piped up, "I have an idea. Will you let us show you in a different way?"

Indi turned her head, wondering what her sister was up to, but saw a gleam in her eye that meant Englan had a plan. She glanced back at Ashley and saw her nodding.

"I will listen, Englan," she mumbled. "I'm not saying I will believe you, but I will listen. You two…well, you are my new sisters, and it's the least I can do."

Englan nodded once. "It will take us some time to get ready, so we will do it next week, okay?" She grabbed Indi, and they dashed out of the room.

CHAPTER 22

THE SHOW

May 2003

"What are you doing?" Indi hissed, pulling against her sister. "What are you planning to show her?"

"A play!" Englan answered. "Think about it, Indi. She's an *actress*. What better way to help her understand than with a play?"

Indi shouted with laughter, "Of course!" *Why hadn't I thought of that?*

Ashley had been acting since she was a young child, and it was the best way to help her see the love of God.

Approaching Ashley as they had done had led to her sharing what had happened to her sister. No wonder she was so bitter and broken. She had lost her sister and turned on God on the same day.

"We have to lead her back, Englan," Indi insisted. "It will change her life."

Englan nodded. "Yep. Now we just have to come up with a script and find people to act in it."

Finding people turned out to be easier than Indi had imagined. At the park, they asked some of their new friends to act in their play. Everyone was surprisingly keen on the idea.

Several of their friends even helped with writing the script. It was a story about Jesus saving a young boy from drowning and then talking to him about dedicating his life to the Lord.

Many parents decorated, sewed costumes, and built sets.

"You're such kind girls that you would even attempt to do this for Ashley," Alyssa expressed to them as the team of four hammered and sawed away, building their teeny stage.

They had set it up in a corner of the park where no one would mind, and they were nearly finished now. Englan had already declared that as soon as it was complete, she planned to paint the whole thing pink.

Indi grinned at the ridiculous thought and then winked up at Alyssa. "This is the least we could do," she responded. "Ashley needs our help, and she's our sister now. We are so excited that she said yes to listening!"

Now, as they put the finishing touches on the stage, she could hardly wait to perform the play. *This* was why they had come to Hollywood; she was certain of it.

In the end, they performed their play there in the park on a bright, moderately warm day that only Southern California could give. It was a short play. In fact, it only lasted thirty minutes. Minimal props were used since they knew that Ashley had attended church when she was younger so she already knew many basic Bible stories.

The youngest boy forgot to come back on stage after he 'drowned,' and Englan had to search for him. She located him on the park swings. Indi was forced to improvise as Jesus, turning water into wine and so forth, until the boy returned. Even with the hiccup, the play ended perfectly. At the completion of the final lines, Indi looked up in time to witness Ashley on her feet, clapping, with tears streaming down her face.

That very night, Ashley accepted Jesus into her life with her parents, Indi, and Englan there to guide her.

CHAPTER 23

NEW MISSION

October 2004

From that day forward, Indi, Englan, and Ashley were the best of friends...and sisters, too, of course!

They had a new mission. They traveled throughout Hollywood, ministering to many actors and actresses who had lost their way, much like Ashley had. They gained access to movie sets with their purpose to share the simple gospel message with as many as would listen. They stood outside, waiting for scenes to wrap. They were alert and available to speak with anyone who was willing to listen. Some days, they would chat with no one. Other days, two or three people walked off a movie set straight to them, looking to find someone who cared to listen.

They scheduled personal meetings with anyone who was interested, encouraged many, and shared ideas on how to remain a steadfast Christian while in the movie business.

"What do you think — will she stick to it?" Ashley asked one night when the three of them stayed up late having another one of their sister slumber parties. A bowl of popcorn was wedged between them — with extra butter for Englan, of course — along with several packages of sweet and sour candy. The girls had taken to having slumber parties at least once a weekend to talk about what had happened during the week.

These parties were also in response to Ashley's constant complaining that she had to sleep in her room alone. To be honest, she slept in the hammock in Indi and Englan's room more often than anywhere else. Indi smiled at the thought and then turned back to Ashley's question. They were discussing a young girl they had met earlier that day — about their age at fifteen — who had seemed truly wild on the set. She had been keenly interested in what the girls had to say about Jesus, and she had even invited them to her house the next day to share more.

"She sure seemed like she wanted to know more," Indi replied, excited. "I mean, the poor girl! Growing up in Hollywood — "

" — Where people expect you to do the most terrible things, even as a teen," Ashley completed Indi's sentence (like sisters often do).

Indi and Englan grinned. This wasn't the first time they had had similar thoughts. Since finding God, Ashley had rerouted her career entirely, accepting only roles that fit her new outlook on life. Not everyone was so blessed, however. Some of the young actors were still being told what to do by their parents or agents and struggled with the idea of pursuing what they wanted versus what their parents wanted.

2007

When Indi and Ashley turned eighteen, they had another 'official' slumber party and decided that they wanted to start taking mission trips to the rest of the world. Englan was eleven and much too young to join in, but then Alyssa volunteered to accompany them. They planned a mission trip every summer to different places. They even returned to London. Indi was a little heartbroken during that trip. She was in London again but without her parents this time. She remembered her daddy's words about them never returning to London again, but then she realized that she was there doing God's work and that He had led her to this place again. Returning to London helped Indi heal a little bit more.

Indi guided Ashley and Englan on a tour of the city. Englan, who did not remember very much about London, was extremely excited that they had returned to the place after which she had been named. Indi shared with Englan the beautiful details their mother had enjoyed when they had visited England as a family. She escorted them to the palaces they had once visited as well as the National Gallery. She steered them to the libraries — her personal favorites — and also to the South Bank to ride the London Eye. In the end, Ashley fell in love with England and declared that they should return annually.

Then one year, they arranged to revisit Indi and Englan's hometown. Indi was particularly nervous. She worried that returning would be too painful — that there would be more memories than she could handle. She even worried that they might find their old house.

However, she realized that if she found their old house, she might be able to obtain some sort of memories from it, and that would be a blessing. She also hoped to visit some of her old friends again.

The first day they arrived, she arranged a friend reunion.

Some of her friends had lost their way, but Indi delighted in the opportunity to bring them back to the straight and narrow path. The first time, of course, it was a bit awkward.

"What do you mean I need to get my life back on track?" Clem asked, scowling. She had blossomed into a beautiful woman, and Indi almost did not recognize her at first glance. However, she learned that her old friend had acquired a range of bad habits, including hanging out with a crowd of people who pressured her into some awful, harmful choices.

"Isn't it obvious, Clem?" Olivia asked, putting a hand on one hip and giving Clem a knowing look. "You barely even talk to us anymore, and when you do, all you talk about is all the trouble you get into! Are you sure those friends of yours are real friends?"

"Yeah, I'm pretty sure I saw that guy Joey spray-painting a building the other day, and he wasn't exactly writing poetry," Victoria added, giggling. Indi giggled with her, unable to stop herself from enjoying the company of her old friends.

She turned back to Clem and tried to be firm and serious. "Clem, I know how hard it can be, growing up without a mom to tell you what to do. I did that, too, remember? But that's not an excuse to turn away from Jesus. That path just leads to pain. Are you truly happy now?"

Clem gave her a long, hard look and then broke down, tears streaming down her face. "No! I've missed you guys so much, but once we lost touch, I just thought…"

"That we didn't love you anymore?" Victoria asked. She reached out and tweaked Clem's arm playfully. "Don't be a goon! Weren't we always there for you, even when you were in trouble at school? Why did you believe that would change?"

Clem shot into Victoria's arms. Indi stood back, grinning from ear to ear. This was even easier than she had hoped; all she had to do was give Clem a reason to open up to her friends again, and the old friendships worked for her.

She turned toward Englan, laughing, and saw her sister smiling, though with a twinge of sadness.

"Still thinking about Aunt Loraine?" Indi asked quietly, taking her hand.

Englan nodded and squeezed Indi's hand tightly. Indi squeezed back. She couldn't blame Englan. They had hoped to reunite their family with Aunt Loraine in India, but it was too painful for them to stay with her. Aunt Loraine reminded them immensely of their mother. While it should have been a comfort to them to find family again, it just wasn't. Even when their aunt had asked them to live with her, they both knew that it was not the path they desired any longer.

They loved Jack and Alyssa and felt as though Ashley was truly their sister. This mission God had given them, the mission they were now fulfilling, was the most important thing.

"We have a new family now," Indi whispered, pointing toward Ashley. "God led us in a new direction. We both are sure it is the right thing."

Englan nodded and painted on a tearful smile while Indi tugged her by her tiny hand toward Ashley. God had placed them into Ashley's family and given them a new vision. Together, the three of them would work throughout the world, seeking to influence kingdoms and nations to love God, love others, and love themselves because God is *LOVE*.

THE END

AUTHOR'S NOTE

I pray that this story influences you to know and love God. God wants us to love our neighbors as ourselves and even to love our enemies, but that is impossible to do when we don't know His great love. I want to encourage you to fall in love with God. Sometimes when a loved one dies, you might feel like God made that person die because God does not love you anymore, but that's just not true. God loves you no matter what. He is for you, not against you. John 10:10 reads that He came to bring life and life abundantly. You can put your trust in Him!

Love,
Spencer Lauren

Made in the USA
Columbia, SC
15 April 2017